THE
McCARTNEY
LEGACY

THE
WIZARD'S TEARS

illustrated by Evaline Ness

THE
WIZARD'S
TEARS

by Maxine Kumin and
Anne Sexton

McGraw-Hill Book Company

New York   St. Louis   San Francisco   Montreal   Toronto

Library of Congress Cataloging in Publication Data

Kumin, Maxine W
   The wizard's tears.

   SUMMARY: The new wizard tries to solve all the
town's problems, but carelessness with his own magic
tears creates a tragedy instead.
   [1.   Fantasy]   I.   Sexton, Anne, joint author.
II.   Ness, Evaline.   III.   Title.
PZ7.K949017Wk   [E]   75-8822
ISBN 0-07-035636-X
ISBN 0-07-035637-8 lib. bdg.

3456789RABP789876

For Caesar and Daisy

EVERYTHING was going wrong in the town of Drocknock. All summer there had been a drought, and the reservoir was drying up. Twenty cows had disappeared from farmer Macadoo's pasture without a trace. And worst of all, the old wizard's spells no longer worked. He could not for the life of him bring rain or find the cows. Moreover, all the people of Drocknock had the chicken pox, and the old wizard could not cure them.

EVEN the mayor was covered with itchy red bumps.

"It's no use," the old wizard said sadly. "My abracadabras are all worn out. And my crystal ball is beyond repair. It's peppered with black and white spots like your old dog. And speaking of old dogs, I wish he wouldn't smile at me all the time. I think he thinks I'm a joke."

"See here," said the mayor, twirling the key to the city on the chain around her neck, "Drocknock needs you. We can't get along without a wizard. And we can't get along without a smiling dog, either. Wise dogs smile, you know."

The water commissioner took off his red hunting cap to scratch some of his chicken pox. "I second the motion," he said. "We need a wizard for our drought."

"Don't worry," said the old wizard. "I've sent for a replacement. And as soon as he gets here, I'll tell him all the town troubles. After that, I'm moving into the Home for Retired Wizards."

THE NEW WIZARD arrived that very afternoon on a red motor bike. The ink was hardly dry on his diploma. He was very young and nervous. He had never been away from home before, and he was lonely already.

"First we must get after the itches," he said bravely, for he was not sure he knew how. But under *Chicken Pox* in the wizard encyclopedia, he read the proper spell for curing red bumps: WATCH THE MOON OVER YOUR SHOULDER, CATCH A BEE IN A JAR AND WASH YOUR FACE WITH BUTTERMILK.

The mayor called a town meeting and the young wizard timidly gave the instructions.

"How clever," said the townspeople. "The old wizard never did anything but recite abracadabra." And they looked at the moon over their left shoulders. Each one caught a bee in a jar, and they all scrubbed their faces with buttermilk. That was the end of the chicken pox.

THE YOUNG WIZARD was an instant success. The people of Drocknock carried him around the town square on their shoulders.

"Thank you, thank you!" he said. "I love you all. I will be the wisest wizard you ever had."

Next he looked up *Cows, disappearing,* in the wizard encyclopedia. It said: TAKE ONE FINGERNAIL PARING AND BURY IT. EAT FIVE PEAS WITH A KNIFE. SAY THE NAMES OF ALL YOUR COWS BACKWARDS.

Farmer Macadoo did as he was told. He had hardly finished pronouncing the last three names—Sseb, Yam and Nna—when the missing cows came single file down the hill into the barn.

"Hot ziggity," said the farmer. "What a wonderful young wizard you are." And he gave a square dance in the barnyard that very night to celebrate the return of his cows.

BUT the mayor took the young wizard aside. "See here," she said. "The drought is our most important problem. We can't wash our clothes or water our gardens anymore."

"I second the motion," said the water commissioner. "We're all thirsty. Everyone is rationed. Nobody can have more than one cup of water a day, and soon that will be gone."

"A drought is hard," the young wizard said doubtfully. And he went home to study the matter in the wizard encyclopedia. There was nothing under droughts. He looked under *Wells, dry*; *Reservoirs*, and then under *Rain, How to Make*.

THERE he found the answer:

BLOW UP ONE HUNDRED BALLOONS AND HANG THEM FROM ONE HUNDRED OWLS' NESTS. COOK ONE THOUSAND AND ONE DAISIES AND EAT THEM AT HIGH NOON. SPRINKLE THE EMPTY RESERVOIR WITH FIVE WIZARD'S TEARS. And then, printed in large red letters, CAUTION: PROCEED WITH CARE.

The mayor and the water commissioner and the wizard blew up balloons until their cheeks sagged. The people of Drocknock shook their heads. "Daisies!" they muttered. "No one eats daisies." But pick them they did and eat them they did, seasoned with lemon juice and cooked in butter.

IT WAS NOT SO EASY for the wizard, however. He sat by the reservoir and thought sad thoughts, but the tears would not come.

"I have a problem," he said. "Drocknock has made me too happy. How can I cry when everyone here loves me?"

He went home and dialed the old wizard. "Old wizard, I am in trouble. I am so happy, I cannot cry the necessary tears for the incantation."

Now the old wizard was wise in the ways of living, even though his abracadabra had worn out. "Peel an onion," he advised. "And the tears will come. But *beware, beware*. Don't overdo it. A wizard's tears are precious. A wizard's tears are powerful. They can make strange magic."

The young wizard peeled an onion and cried ten tears into a teacup. Five of these he sprinkled into the empty reservoir, and the rains came just as promised. It rained for five days and five nights. The umbrella shop did a big business. The reservoir filled and there was water for everyone.

THE TOWNSPEOPLE were so grateful that they gave a roller-skating party in the town square. The band played the Skaters' Waltz and everyone whizzed around in pairs.

THE NEXT MORNING the young wizard looked at the five remaining tears in the teacup by his bed. He forgot the old wizard's warning. "Powerful tears, what can you do for me?" he asked. "Can you serve me my breakfast in bed?"

He dipped in his finger and blew the tears one by one into the air. *Beware, beware!* sang in his head, but he paid no attention. At once a magnificent breakfast appeared on a giant-size tray. There was orange juice, waffles, sausages, coffee, and a piece of chocolate cake. The tears even knew he was partial to chocolate cake.

It was such a beguiling breakfast that the wizard decided he would order one every morning. That night he peeled an onion and tucked it under his pillow. *When I wake up tomorrow*, he thought, *I will cry into the teacup and conjure up another fine feast.*

BUT the wizard had a restless night. Every time he turned on his pillow the smell of the onion tickled his nose and tears ran down his cheeks in his sleep. By dawn the bed was as wet as a bathmat. He sat up on the soggy sheets, but although he closed his eyes and pressed his fingers to his temples, the breakfast tray did not appear.

"Oh dear," he wondered. "What have I done with my precious wizard's tears? Have I used up my magic? Why didn't I listen to the warnings, *beware*, *beware*? Maybe the old wizard can tell me." And he hurried out to the red motor bike.

ON the way to the old wizard's, he met the big yellow school
bus. It was stalled in the middle of the road. Frogs peered
out at him from every window.

What's going on here? he asked himself. But there was
no one to answer. Inside his head a little voice repeated,
beware, beware!

AT the next corner he pulled into the gas station. At the pump there squatted a large green frog. There was no one to fill his tank. *Beware, beware.*

Fearing disaster, he hurried off to the mayor's house to tell her the strange happenings.

IN the mayor's kitchen two frogs sat on the table. One wore the key to the city around its neck. The other peeked out from under the water commissioner's red hunting cap. "Croak, croak!" they said as he entered.

"OH DEAR! What have I done to Drocknock?" cried the young wizard. "Have I bewitched the whole town with my tears?" He put the two frogs in his pocket to keep them safe and ran out into the street for help. But every house and shop contained nothing but frogs. There was no one left in the town of Drocknock but the mayor's old dog.

The young wizard walked up and down the frog-filled streets. How lonely he was! There was no one to talk to.

"I must hurry to the old wizard," he said. "Maybe he has an abracadabra. Maybe he can help me undo this evil sorcery."

"LOOK what happened," he said to the old wizard. And he took the two frogs out of his pocket. "This is the mayor and this is the water commissioner."

"I told you beware. Wizard's tears are precious. Wizard's tears are powerful. They must never be used for breakfast in bed," said the old wizard when he had heard the sad story.

"And I was so happy in Drocknock," said the young wizard.

The old wizard took pity on him and gave him a riddle to undo the strange sorcery. "Guess the answer to this riddle and your town will fill up with people again," he told him. "What is white with black spots in the daytime and black with white spots at night? The answer is under your nose. Guess the answer in three days, and Drocknock will be itself again."

THE YOUNG WIZARD hurried back to town. He took the mayor and the water commissioner out of his pocket and set them down very gently at the edge of the reservoir. He didn't know the answer to the riddle yet, but he did know that frogs needed water.

All afternoon he went from house to house collecting frogs and stacking them in his wheelbarrow. He carried them to the reservoir and put them carefully, one by one, at the water's edge. They all croaked and jumped into the mud. As he worked, the young wizard repeated the riddle: "What is white with black spots in the daytime and black with white spots at night?"

"I have it!" He hurried to the phone. "Old wizard, I have it! The answer is a newspaper."

"NO," said the old wizard. "That's not it. The answer is right under your nose." And he hung up with a click.

"Oh, I'm so lonely," said the young wizard. "If only there were someone to talk to. The mayor is a wise woman. She would help me think of the answer to the riddle, but now she is only a frog." And he was so sad that he cried some real tears. Presto! there was an elegant breakfast before him, complete with chocolate cake. But he was too sad to eat. He fed the cake to the dog, who wagged his tail and smiled.

The next day the young wizard woke up with a new guess in his head. He hurried to call the old wizard. "I have it!" he said. "The answer is a birch tree."

"NO," said the old wizard. "That's not it. The answer is right under your nose."

The young wizard spent another lonely day. At the reservoir the frogs croaked in chorus.

The next morning he had another guess. "A blueberry muffin!" he cried to the old wizard. And again the old wizard said, "No. That's not it. The answer is right under your nose. You have until sunset to save Drocknock." And again the phone went click.

SADLY the young wizard walked down to the reservoir once more. He sat on a log and listened to the frogs, and the old dog sat at his feet. They sat silently all day, a miserable pair. The sun was beginning to go down in the afternoon sky. The wizard tried to keep from crying, but the true tears came thick and fast, and with them came breakfast after breakfast, neatly stacked on enormous trays at the water's edge. Even the old dog was sad and did not beg for chocolate cake.

"I'M not much of a wizard," he said to the dog. "I can't even guess the answer to a riddle. Here you are, just an old spotted dog, but I bet you could do better than I can. You with all your black spots. Come to think of it, you look like a newspaper. Come to think of it, you look like a birch tree. Come to think of it, you even look like a blueberry muffin! That's it, that's it! What is white with black spots in the daytime and black with white spots at night? A Dalmatian dog is! A spotted Dalmatian dog!"

AND BEFORE HIS VERY EYES the frog wearing the key around its neck turned back into the mayor. The frog wearing the red hunting cap turned back into the water commissioner. The gas station woman and farmer Macadoo and all the townspeople came out of the water in their old shapes.

"SEE here," said the mayor, after the young wizard had told her the whole story. "That will be enough of that. No more breakfasts in bed for you. No more onions under the pillow."

"I'm starved," said the water commissioner. "I think I will eat this breakfast."

"Me, too," said farmer Macadoo. And they all gathered around to eat.

"Chocolate cake," said the mayor. "That's my favorite breakfast." And she forgave the young wizard his foolish tears.

I will never be lonely again!
Drocknock is the place for me!

AND the mayor's dog smiled his old smile.

THE AUTHORS

Maxine Kumin and the late **Anne Sexton** are both widely known for their adult poetry. Mrs. Kumin won the 1973 Pulitzer Prize for Poetry, and Mrs. Sexton was awarded the 1967 Pulitzer Prize for Poetry. They were close friends who enjoyed collaborating on books for young people.

Maxine Kumin has written over a dozen children's books, including the SEE AND READ STORYBOOKS IN VERSE series for Putnam, and THE BEACH BEFORE BREAKFAST, nominated for the Caldecott and illustrated by Leonard Weisgard. She is also the author of several adult novels.

Anne Sexton received many honors for her work. Along with Mrs. Kumin, she wrote two SEE AND READ SCIENCE BOOKS, also for Putnam, as well as JOEY AND THE BIRTHDAY PRESENT for McGraw-Hill.

THE ARTIST

A distinguished author in her own right, **Evaline Ness** has illustrated many outstanding books for young people, including JOEY AND THE BIRTHDAY PRESENT. Miss Ness grew up in Pontiac, Michigan, and attended art schools in Chicago, Washington, D.C., New York, and Italy. The recipient of the Caldecott medal for SAM, BANGS & MOONSHINE, Miss Ness also has three Caldecott runners-up to her credit: TOM TIT TOT, A POCKETFUL OF CRICKET, and ALL IN THE MORNING EARLY.